WILL YOU BE MY EVER AFTER ?

PART - 1

HIMANSHU K. TIWARI

"This book is dedicated to everyone who is on a search for a happily ever after."

"Also to the ones, who found their's."

"Cheers !"

Contents

Preface

The book is all about the journey of two people, finding the meaning of love in their lives. While growing up, we have read a lot of fictions and fantasies with the ending stated as..... "and they lived happily ever after", almost every time. But is it the truth? Is this what happens in reality too ? I believe it depends on what you consider as a " happy ever after " . In the upcoming pages, you will witness the lives of Anirudh and Radhika; two different yet similar beings. This is the first part of their story.

Acknowledgements

Everything in this book has been written by the "reader" within me. Hope you relate. Big hugs to the people without whom, both; this book and my life would'nt be possible. My mom, dad and their devoted love. You two make me believe that soulmates exist!

CHAPTER ONE

Room No. 42

It was a late winter night when Shyam heard a soft sobbing sound coming from the other side of the corridor. He kept ignoring it until it became quite bothersome and he thought of approaching towards the source of this agony. When he tracked it down, he found himself standing at the door of room no. 42. The room was belonged to Anirudh Kashyap , a 23 year old with a slight brownish complexioned , 5"8 inced boy. Anirudh was a little introvert when it came to hanging out with other people but he usually interacted well with anyone who approached to have a conversation. Shyam and Anirudh were both in the final year of their B.tech and already possesed good placements with a decent package. But still they had to get the degree and pass out for the sake of getting the jobs. Although Anirudh was not a high scorer who aced in all the subjects but still he was also not that bad that he could suffer with anxiety attacks while panicking about passing the exam. So clearly the sobbing had nothing to do with the exams.

"AABE KASHYAP TU RO RAHA HAI KYA " (Hey Kashyap are you crying?) Shyam said while knocking . Just as he asked , the sound disappeared. Perhaps Anirudh tried to convince Shyam that like the other students of the hostel he was also in a deep sleep. But both of them knew that he wasn't. " ACCHA CHAL KHOL , MAI JAANTA HU TU SO TOH NAI RAHA HAI " (Okay , open the door: I know you ain't sleeping.) Shyam again made an attempt to enter the room. He knocked a several times but neither the door was opening and nor Anirudh was replying to anything he said. Therefore Shyam decided to go back to his bed and as he turned and started walking; he heard the opening of the catch. He turned back and saw a messed up Anirudh at the door. He invited Shyam to come inside with a nod of his head. Shyam came inside and Anirudh locked the door again. He told Shyam to settle on the bed and he grabbed a stool for himself to sit upon. Anirudh sat in front of him and his partially swollen eyes which certainly were the result of weeping enough and his messy hair would have made anyone aware of him not being well. But still Anirudh managed to put a pale smile and maybe it was his last attempt in dragging Shyam to believe that he was alright. But within minutes of sitting by his side, Shyam figured out that something dreadful is bothering this person. He could tell that by the condition in which the room was. Anirudh was a very sorted kind of guy and he always kept his room as well as his belongings systematically. But this time the room didn't seemed to be Anirudh's . The crumpled bedsheet, the displaced books told something else. By every passing minute Shyam became a bit more concerned about what was happening with him. " Is everything alright ? " Shyam moved his hand keeping it on Anirudh's shoulder. Perhaps this friendly gesture was enough to let him through the fake portrail of everything going all right. Anirudh broke down; and this time the sobbing had turned into wailing. Shyam had never seen him like this, The image he had of Anirudh was of a boy who although was not that good in socialising but had a very positive aura around him. He was very passionate when it came to learning new things and never stepped back in the mid way. But this Anirudh was quite different. "You did‘nt lose your practical file, did you ? " Shyam asked. Anirudh’s wailing had led him to think of all the possible centres from where his breakdown could have possibly emerged. But Anirudh was not answering to anything and kept crying with his head down. After another couple of minutes of crying he finally uttered "I don’t think he’s gonna make it this time....he is too old now and this..... it’s the second time.....it’s just too much for him". A confused yet concerned Shyam looked at Anirudh as he muttered. At this point of time, Shyam’s mind was filled with numerous questions but he did asked the first among them all; "Who?" After a pause, Anirudh clearified, "Dadu...."

"What ? did he have it again? "

"Yes, this morning, while he was going to the bathroom he felt a severe chest pain and he fell on the ground. This is the second time he is having the attack; thats just.....too much for his aged body"

Anirudh’s father passed away when he was in Std 7th ; after two years his mother also left him after having a 8 months fight with colorectal cancer. Although the chance of survival for a patient of colorectal cancer is said to be at 63% . But Anirudh believed that her illness was just an excuse and his mother wasn’t alive since her husband was gone. After they both left , his Dadu was all Anirudh had as family. Although he had an uncle and an aunt, but they treated him like anything but family. It was like his aunt had her own dictionary of words; mostly abusive she used on Anirudh yet he found them to be creative . Though his uncle never said anything to his face but often backstabbed him with his wife in front of anyone who came to their house. Usually Anirudh didn't took any of these solemnly but sometimes things got a bit out of hand like this one time when his aunt accused him of stealing a phone which probably she hid by herself. At times like these; his Dadu came to his rescue and stood by him. He was like a relief among all the chaos. A friend who always helped him to make her aunt's conspirecies for making his life miserable go abortive. But somewhere his Dadu also knew that he could'nt be there with him forever. Therefore he sent Anirudh to Gwalior to complete his engineering that'll perhaps help him to stand at his own feet and be self sufficient. Earlier this year he suffered with a heart attack and this was the second time it happened to him. Somewhere, a hidden fear had struck Anirudh that he would lose his grandfather as well.

Shyam tried to calm Anirudh down but he also knew that nothing is going to work and he needed to see his Dadu and maybe that 'll give him some soet of relief. Therefore he suggested Anirudh to do the same. " You know you need to go there , meet him ", he said.

"Do you really think that i didn't thought of doing it, Infact it was the foremost thought in my mind"

"Then what's stopping you? "

Anirudh got up from the stool and walked towards his study table, he grabbed an old looking diary from there. He turned some pages and once he stopped ; a little smile appeared below his teary eyes. Shyam also got up from the bed anxiously to have a look at the reason behind that smile on that wailing face. He saw that among those pages lied a grainy and a bit tattered polaroid of Anirudh and his grandfather. Anirudh seemed to be a 12 year old in that picture , giving the camera perhaps his bestest smile that showed probably all his teeth.

"We took this while we were at the Saras Mela " said Anirudh , with his eyes still on that picture as if he wanted to elope in that time again like a toddler.

"When I was leaving for Delhi, Dadu handed me this and said to have a look at it incase I miss him a lot. But also warned me not to think of returning back to him until I do something satisfactory with my life. He swore to me."

Shyam looked at Anirudh and realised that he had never seen him smiling so carelessly like he was in the polaroid.

"I know you guys made some kind of promise but I also know that your Dadu loves you way more than you do and he must be craving to see you as much as you are. And right now I think that seeing each other would be the best thing for both of you and every thing else is irrelevant." Shyam said.

Perhaps , these were the words Anirudh needed to hear and at that moment every other thought, fear and consequence blurred in his mind and the next thing he wanted to do was to see his Dadu.

He clasped Shyam like it was a way to thank him for doing what he had done.The second thing he did was pulled out his phone from the pocket and booked the ticket.

CHAPTER TWO

The train to Gwalior

Anirudh boarded the first train to Gwalior the upcoming day. He didn't bothered what seats he got , whether the reservation was confirm or was in RAC. While he was in the rickshaw on his way to the station, Anirudh had hypothetically practiced all the possible scenarios that can occur with him in the train. If he didn't get a place to sit he was mentally prepared to stand and cover the 7 hours of the journey. If he missed the train, then he would......"No! No! missing the train is not an option....." he told himself. He wanted to be there as soon as he could get.

But most of his wild themed scenarios remained hypothetical only as he got a decent seat in the train. Also the coach was rarely congested and there were not much people as it was not a season in which people usually travel a lot. Beside Anirudh, the window seat was occupied by a fairly old lady; most must in her mid 70s . Anirudh didn't had a proper look at her face; he only had a glance while he was sitting. And now he found it a bit awkward as well as kind of graceless to turn his head 90 degrees and stare at her. Also he was too coy to have a small talk with her. Therefore he just reclined on his seat the way he was, with his eyes closed and thought of relaxing a bit and have some final moments of peace which he was sure of not getting in near future amidst the taunts and cuss he was soon going to receive from his aunt. He was pondering all these when he heard . 'These things don't work when you need them the most' she was murmuring. Anirudh tried to keep his eyes shut and ignore her. 'Excuse me?' she poked him with her fist and that made it quite hard for him to keep up with his ignoring. 'Yes?' he said as if he was busy minding his own business and now the old lady had disturbed him, although he had his ears on everything the lady was saying, but still.

' My son taught me how to do a video call , before coming to the station ; But you see this damn phone doesn't seem to work the way it was earlier' she clarified the issue.

'Maybe it's a network thing' he said , stretching his hand indicating the lady to hand over her phone in order to have a look at it.

But instead the lady gave him a mere frown and pulled the phone a bit more closer to her; denying to give it to him. The situation became quite awkward and to break the silence he finally spoke.

'Well if you know the phone number, you can use my phone instead'

That brought a smile on her face and she made the call from his mobile phone. While she was talking at the top of her voice. Anirudh had to atone for the disturbance caused by her chat.

While he kept his own resentment hidden behind a facade and was facing the other passengers who by then were already annoyed by the lady's chat and most probably thought that Anirudh was related to her so were giving him scunnered looks; the lady poked him again. She handed back his phone to him and reclined on her seat with a sense of satisfaction on her face, totally unaware of the discomfiture caused by her.On her behalf, Anirudh again gave an assuring smile to everyone and declared that the hostility had ended. Due to the anxiousness, Anirudh had deprived sleep last night so he started feeling a bit drowsy and eventually he dozed off.

The train was at full steam when he woke up to the cacophony caused by the hawkers who were constantly roaming in and out of the coach. He was sluggish but managed to have a look at his wrist watch. Then with a big yawn he turned towards the window with his mouth still wide open. The lady wasn't there and seat was vacant. Maybe she got off the train while he was busy snoozing. Though he expected atleast a thank you from her but he compensated it with the window seat and with a quick skid he shifted there. He leaned on the window and kept gazing at everything the train passed by. Although he had his eyes there but his mind was on a constant disquisition. He kept calculating everything a several times and everytime tried to conclude things at a positive end. But perhaps the antipathy for his relatives kept resisting him from doing so. He tried thinking that maybe his uncle had also missed him or maybe his aunt will not create a fuss about him being there or atleast they will pretend to do so. But somewhere he knew that he was just bluffing himself and giving false hopes.

Coming out of the station, he felt like a quitter. While he was leaving for Delhi, he had mixed up feelings; part of him was an enraged young lad who was furious about leaving his Dadu and going to some other city, how was all this going to be any good for him. On the other hand he also wanted to do something good and achieve something decent in life and he would have made a bollywood style comeback after that. Like the heroes in the movies seem to do. He would've entered through the main door as a classy gentleman dressed up in a three piece Armani holding a briefcase and maybe a pair of specs and a french cut to apotheosize. Seeing his aunty's face after see had seen him like this would have been worth the separation and if not for all this; he would have done this to make his Dadu proud. But this was nothing identical to either of the situations and this made it worse for him. He had'nt brought much stuff with him, it was just all his necessities that barely filled a bagpack. So instead of standing and waiting for any auto to arrive he thought of taking a stroll down his down. Also the autowala would've charged him excessively.

CHAPTER THREE

From where it all Started

As he was walking, he contemplated every shop that appeared on the way, streets and even some of the houses. It was like him walking down the memory lane. As if it was the whole city was a throwback to all kinds of memories he had there. The remembrance made him simper at times.

Eventually he reached where he was supposed to; his house. The main door was a rusty ironed one that was unoiled from an unknown period, perhaps the gate was more antique than the whole house itself. Dadu had been planning to change the main gate from a very long time but it all just remained a notion and in his defence he used to say that they don't build such quality stuff now. He lifted the handle in order to enter, and that made a creaking sound. This sound was like an indication that someone had arrived and as a child, Anirudh used to make assumptions about who ll be coming based on the intensity of the creak.

'Who's there ? ' he heard his uncle 's voice who was approaching the gate.

' It's me ' Anirudh replied.

He was half way through the gate and he saw his uncle standing in front of him.

‘ Ani?, Is that you ’ His uncle reconfimed adjusting his spectacles on his nose. In his reply, Anirudh gave him a smile.

‘ Are you having a holiday ? , you should’ve informed about your visit ’ his uncle said trying take the baggage from his shoulders.

‘ No...No it’s fine...’ Anirudh spurned.

‘ Actually, I am here to see Dadu...How’s he doing? ’

‘ O yes... you must be worried about him..but you don’t need to...he is actually doing alright ’, his uncle replied in a low tone.

‘ Anyway, it’s good you’re here ,go and meet him..he there in his room ’ he patted his shoulders and smiled at him.

Anirudh had‘nt presumed this unforeseen behaviour his uncle showed. Did one of his assumptions had turned to be right? Did his uncle actually missed him? or maybe it’s all just a formality because he had seen him after a long time and was pretending the entire conversation.

’ Your aunty has gone to her friend’s , she’ll be home by the evening ‘ he answered Anirudh’s unbid query.

He stood behind the door of the room closed his eyes and exhaled for a bit, though he was dying to meet Dadu but he also wanted to be prepared for his anger which may outburst , acknowledging that his dear grandson instead of preparing for his finals, took a break mid-sem.

Anirudh eased the door and sneaked inside.Dadu was taking a siesta perhaps after his lunch. Seeing him sleep so comfortably gave Anirudh a strange contentment. He had thought that he will clasp in his arms the moment he will see him. But right now, he just wanted to stand there or maybe sit beside him and enjoy the delectation on Dadu’s face. He wasn’t sure about the reason behind it, but he also didn’t cared about that much either. He held his hand gently and that touch took him straight way to that 12 year old boy who was there in the polaroid, He eyes filled with tears. He thought of himself to be a little selfish for not being here for Dadu. He squeezed his eyes shut and a drop of tear rolled down from his cheek to his grandfather's hand.

He woke up. 'Ani?' he said, with a wrinkled forehead.

Anirudh wiped his cheek instantaneously.

' Before you start scolding me...you should know....' He tried to speak but couldn't complete because Dadu hugged him and Anirudh finally became a teenager again. He just closed his eyes and relished.They both were so overwhelmed with emotions that none of them wanted to let go the other one. Shyam was right, they both craved for this!

'How are you Dadu?'

'As fine as a horse, have a look yourself'

'Don't lie...i know about the attack, I was worried...'

'Worried...that i ll die?'

'You make it sound worse'

'Well you see...your Dadi used to stay that i am a pretty obstinate man, don't worry I am not going anywere before telling your children how there father used to cry for ice-creams when you will be prohibiting them from having one' he smirked. Anirudh hugged him back.

'I missed you' he sighed.

'Me too' he patted his back.

' Oh, so you're here ! ', a harsh but familiar voice hit his ears from behind. He had already guessed who was it before turning.

' Namaste chachi ' He greeted his aunt who was standing at the door.

' You should have informed atleast! '

' Well it was all so quick, I didn't get the time to' , said Anirudh.
' So you thought, we weren't taking good care of your Dadu! therefore you came here to verify , isn't it? ', she questioned over.
' It's not that....', he hushed.
' I wanted to see him, so gave him a call ', Dadu interrupted. His aunt gave him a stare and marched downstairs.
' Is it weird if i say that I quite missed her too? ', Anirudh said with a straight face and they both chuckled.
A bunch of memories were recalled and a number of talks were shared among the two of them, afterwards. Since Anirudh was exhausted from the journey; he passed out and had an undisturbed slumber beside his Dadu later.
His uncle and aunt were never able to conceive. They decided to keep the reason private and the family respected that. Whenever asked, their simplest answer was given that it was their mutual decision not to have a baby. But little Anirudh always thought that it was due to that one time when his aunty slapped him so hard that he almost lost a tooth. The livid boy knew that he could do nothing to take his revenge therefore he cursed that she never has a baby because she didn't know how to treat a child and she may kill it. But he also regretted it when there were times when some distant relatives used to poke the fact so much that his aunt ended up crying. He felt guilty of cursing her when he saw her weeping. But it was only until he became old enough to understand how pregnencies work and that gave him sort of relief. Then he knew that he'd been feeling guilty of a sin that he never committed. Thank God!
The dinner table felt like an examination centre. Everyone knew each other but they were'nt talking. Juast busy minding their own stuff. There was utmost silence. None of

them spoke. The only audible thing was the clinking of the spoons and cutlery. And there was a point when the silence became unbearable for Anirudh as he was'nt used to such dead quiteness while eating. He was just about to drown when his phone beeped.

SHYAM COLLEGE

"Hey! Reached?"

Anirudh B.TECH

"Yup, the train was on time"

SHYAM COLLEGE

" How's he doing? "

Anirudh B.TECH

"He's Good"

SHYAM COLLEGE

"NICE. BTW Don't worry about the assignments. I'll manage"

Anirudh B.TECH

Thanks Bh....

"Ahem, ahem"

Anirudh looked up at his uncle who coughed and he realised that his constant clatter was pretty annoying. ' I'm sorry ', he apologised in a low tone and slid his phone inside.

CHAPTER FOUR

The Girl on the bus stop

Although Anirudh had spent a major part of his life in Delhi, but he always had his heart in Gwalior. As they say, you can take a man out of his hometown but you can never take out the hometown out of the man. Inspite of being in Delhi; he was never able to transform into a proper Delhite and he didn't even attempted to. Though he acquired some things that were necessary for survival. Raising the voice amidst a quarrel and yelling " TU JAANTA NAHI MERA BAAP KAUN HAI! " was one of them. He wanted to have a saunter down the streets so he went for one. The roads felt like a toy store to him and as he wandered his excited eyes gazed at each and every corner. It was not like he went to places where he had never been to, but the excitement he had was just uncanny. He strolled for quite a time and searched for the thelas from where he used to eat someimtes. He found some of them and searched for the other ones at every spot he could remember. His legs started to give up and as he was looking around for a place to sit his eyes got the hold of a bus stand across the road.
" *DAMN IT! YEH BHI GAYA !!* ", he sat there for probably a minute when the expletive ringed his ears. He looked up

and all he could see was this girl , barely of 25 ; standing two hands away from him. She had these big earrings dangling on her ears but the scarf around her face kept Anirudh from seeing her face. She had a phone in her hand that she continuosly patted and shaked as if it would make it alive. Maybe the sentence was regarding her phone going off. For a moment, he thought of interupting but he was too shy to talk to her or just ask her if everything was alright.While he was busy having this self-debate about how to have a conversation with her. She snapped her fingers right in front of his nose.

'Excuse Me?', she said.

Before he could figure out the first question she fired one more at him.

' Do you know how can I get to Dwarkapuri? ', the exclamation in her voice turned interrogative.

And that was the moment when he looked into her deep eyes. And this time even his diffidence couldn't forbid him from holding his eyes on her. He kept looking at her frowned eyes motionlessly. Her eyes portraied a different kind of harmony. And in that moment he understood what it is like to drown into someone's eyes. Till then he just thought that to be a poetic metaphor.

' Hello? Do you understand? ' , she snapped again.

And with that snap she broke the spell she had casted on him unknowingly.

'You can take a bus if you want to', Anirudh tried to be as subtle as he could.

' OKAY ',and she turned around and continued with her tapping. She kept looking at the vehicles passing by and her anxiousness could be easily deprived by the way she tapped her feet and clunched her fists constantly.

' You know from where you'll get the bus right? ' asked

Anirudh.
'ACTUALLY I DON'T, AND I DON'T EVEN LIKE TO ASK THAT FROM A RANDOM STRANGER '
She finally lost her patience and her words turned a bit blaring. But just then she might understood the fact that he was not the idle person to be victimzed.
' I'm sorry ', she sighed and sat on a bench that was parallel to Anirudh's.
For a few minutes she just sat there silently with her head leaned back and kept her eyes closed. And Anirudh was unable to figure out that how should he respond to the scenario. What is it that people usually say in these type of situations? or maybe he should just get away and pretend that he never had this awkward interaction. But he wanted to say something to her :calm her down.
' It's okay ' he broke the silence.
' Well, I kinda know what it's like to roam in an unknown city. Been there, done that ', he continued.
She opened her eyes and looked at him. Anirudh smiled.
' I am Anirudh ', he said
"Radhika"
' I should'nt have shouted on you. I m sorry. ', she apologised again.
' Don't worry about that told you ', he tried to lessen her guilt.
' Thanks by the way, you can carry on with your stuff, I'll figure something out ', she told him.
' Well, I can walk with you to the bus ', he said but shortly realised that it was something that you would not usually expect from a stranger to say.
' I mean if you want to....' he added quickly before it could add more awkwardness to their coversation. But she had already read his discomfiture.

‘ Is that too much to ask from a guy you’ve just met? ’ she replied with a glee in order to ease things for him.
‘ Of course, not ’, he replied back and they both stood up.

CHAPTER FIVE

Strangers

Their stroll was rather silent.

Unlike other boys of his age, Anirudh did not had a collection of catchy pick-up lines, which he could have used as conversation starters. Also he didn't want to sound stupid by saying anything unrequired.

Radhika; on the other hand was more of a talkative person, she liked to speak out her mind.

'You don't talk much, do you? ',she spoke to break the silence

' Kind of, I mean my friends say so too ', he replied.

' Are you new here? ' he asked

' Well, technically yes. I am from Dehradun but my aunt lives here; although I am not among her frequent visitors. It's just that I wanted to spend some time away from home.'

' So it's kind of a getaway for you.'

' You can put it that way too. I mean its strange how people feel that they matter the most and are always thinking that the world revolves around them. I think we need a time to time reality check that reminds us that things aren't the way we usually put and there is a lot more out there. Travelling does that to you. '

' Oookayyy... I think it would take me some time to process that. '

‘ You see, I know sometimes I sound a lot more intellectual than I look, you can say that if you want to; I’ll take it as a compliment. ’

‘ Agreed ’

‘ OKAY, you’ve heard much about me, so whats your story? ’, Radhika’s eyes lit up with excitement.

‘ Well, I don’t have a rousing story; I live in Delhi ’

‘ So, why are you here ? anything specific or it’s just pure wanderlust ? ’

‘ It’s the city I was born in and my family lives here, I came to see them. ’

‘ Ohhhhh...’

And their words came to an end again and once more silence sweeped in.

‘ I think the vehicles have increased.... I mean it used to be quiter place back then ’

This time Anirudh took the charge and tried to talk but Radhika said nothing and just nodded her head in affirmation.

‘ Hey did you notice, our feets are in sync ’

Anirudh bent his head to have a view of this discovery of hers.

‘ Uff, you just messed it ’,

The annoyance in her words made him believe that he must have done something unlawful.

The more time they were spending, it was getting difficult for Anirudh to figure her out. At times her perceptions would be full of things that made him wonder about his own ways of looking the world but just then she would say something imbicile enough to have a laugh or atleast share a smile.

Some people carry a positive aura with them. It’s like an unapperent bubble, they are always surrounded with and

you can feel it when you're around.
Radhika was one of them for sure.
' Here you go ' , Anirudh pointed at the bus.
Though Radhika was relieved that finally she 'll be home, she wanted to have a bit more of this conversation. Anirudh on his side, wanted the same. But both of them were rather too coyed too admit that. This unexpected meeting was somehow relished by both of them.
' So I guess, that's it ', Radhika's words came out with a hushed tone.
' Yup ',
' Can I have your number ? ', both of them said in one breath and then chuckled.
' Well.... isn't it kinda weird to ask for a girl's number with whom you've just met! ', Radhika smirked.
' Totally ' Anirudh nodded.
' Give me yours.... i'll see if I get the time. you,ll get mine ', she teased.
The clock strucked 3. It was almost morning
But Anirudh didn't had a minute of sleep. His eyes, wide open, were just staring nowhere , the ticking of the clock was the only audible sound in the room. Though he was a bit resented by the fact that Radhika had not contacted him yet but his inner self was constantly objecting him with reasons that could have possibly retained her from doing so. He wasn't able to recall the last time when something so petty like this had bothered him to such an extent. Though he was annoyed but at the same time he enjoyed the waiting too. The excitement had held him on his toes. It was quite amusing in a peculiar way. He plugged his earphone in, played a song and closed his eyes.
Little did he knew he was not the only one having a scrimmage with sleep.

Radhika was also awake. Lying on her bed, staring on the lock screen of her phone. ‘ No new notifications’, It said. She unlocked her phone and howered her finger over her Mom’s contact number but never dialled it. She repeated this for a couple of times then finally threw her phone to the other side of the bed.

She buried her head in the pillow and tried closing her eyes as tight as she could until she heard a knock on the door.

" Are you still up? ", her aunt asked peeping inside the room.

She tried to fake her sleep and replied in a drowsy voice, " So are you ?", she said.

Her aunt approached towards her bed and sat near her pillow. She then gently laid her hands on her hair and caressed her.

" So she didn’t called ? ", she queried in a soft voice.

Rahika nodded sideways and shifted her head on her aunt’s lap.

" Maybe she did'nt wanted to " , her voice started breaking.

" It’s not that dear, something else must’ve came up ", her aunt tried to console her.

She rested her head on her aunt’s lap and her aunt kept caressing her.

In this world, everyone I guess has a fair share of messed up things going on in their lives. Some are just good at hiding. We indeed are a generation full of repressed emotions.

Radhika, for her age had already gone through a lot. A teenager may have to face a whole heap of distressing decisions but having to choose among one’s own parents is something really dreadful. Despite of having almost everything ; a girl of her age would’ve died for ; She always had a void that nothing in this world could fill. Her parents ; busy in their own quarrels, never had the time for which their daughter craved. Soon their arguments turned into fierce disputes which later were drawn from their house into the courtroom. Both accused each other of cheating and claimed on every priced possesion which could be divided. The only thing that remain uncalled was Radhika. Unlike most of the divorce cases it was clear that none of them wanted to have her or maybe their new partners wanted so. Radhika always had this fear of not being able to see her parents again or for the least not being able to get the love back from them. She always tried hard to be the reason that tied their family together, but eventually she was seeing all that fading away in front of her eyes. It was when her aunt decided that the little girl needs a break from all that and therefore she called her to Gwalior to stay with her. It was almost a week she had been in Gwalior and everyday she hoped that perhaps her mom or dad will call her to say that they miss her and want her back and if not that; then atleast they will ask how she was. But all she was getting in return of her longings was dissapointment. Among all this, it was a matter of doubt that she would have remembered anything about a boy she just met this evening.

CHAPTER SIX

The First Call

Earphones plugged in, the song still playing; Anirudh rubbed his eyes and looked at the clock with half-opened eyes. It was late enough for his aunt to start fussing. As he pulled the wires out of his ears and sweeped his feet on the floor in search of his slippers, he heard her voice coming from the hall, " He must be up all night watching some movie , these hostel kids I tell you!". He quickly got up from the bed and marched out of the room to mark his presence. Aunty stopped the blabbering to give him an eye and then continued with her stuff. His uncle sitting on the sofa, sipping tea from the cup greeted him good morning. To which he replied with a quick nod and made his way to Dadu's room.

Dadu as expected was awake long before, lying on his bed. Going through the pages of ' Dainik Jagran ' , which he must have already read a few times before since morning.

" How do you manage to get up so early ", Anirudh lied on the sofa beside the bed.

Dadu peeped his head from the newspaper to have a look at him.

" Just like you try to sleep early but fail, I try to get up late in the morning but fail. They say old habits die hard but I think in my case I'll take my habits to death with me. ",

Dadu replied.

" Don't start with your death theories again ", Anirudh said and stretched his legs on the sofa.

" They don't let me go to my morning walks also "

" You've done a lot of walking , there's nothing new left to see here . Get over with your treatments and I'll take you to Delhi with me "

" Huuuhh...You keep your Delhi to yourselves only. I am happy here, Besides I don't want to spend my last moments in an unfamiliar place."

" You are not going to stop that, are you "

Overall speaking, his morning was an average one, until now. Then the cell phone vibrated flashing an unknown number on the screen. His heart skipped a beat and this time he was quite sure of hearing a familiar voice from the other end. He clasped the phone in his hand and rushed to the balcony, praying that the ring does not goes off . He held his breath for a second and then answered the phone.

" He.....hello ? " he mumbled.

" Do you usually pick up this late or this was on purpose ? "

" Well....I wasn't....like expecting your call "

" Ya right ",

And they both went quite for a bit waiting for the other to say something and make this call less awkward.

"HELLO ??", both of them spoke at once and then laughed.

" You first ", said Anirudh

" Well, I was wondering.... if you were like doing anything today?", Radhika completed the sentence slowly.

" NO!! NO!! I am all free ", Anirudh replied excitedly

" Ohhkayy... I got it; needless of you to yell like that"

" Oh I am Sorry...It's the network you know , it's always off here so i thought that maybe..."

" Well, It seems fine to me now, so spare my ears "

" So where are we going ?? "

" Considering the fact that you already assumed that we are going somewhere..."

" I mean...like what's the plan ..."

" You are the native...so aren't you supposed to suggest me places that I, as a tourist should visit ?" Radhika was enjoying Anirudh's child like excitement over the call.

" Ummm...okay..so let me think "

" Go for the best you can "

" Gwalior Fort ? Ever been there ?

" Heard about it, but never got the chance to have a visit"

" SO IT'S DONE THEN ??? "

" Easy..Im wearing earphones"

" Oh sorry...right..I mean if you want to ? "

" Gwalior Fort it is "

" So when and where are we meeting ? "

" See me at the bus stop , at 4 "

" Okay , sounds fine to me "

" Fine "

And there was silence again. They were out of topics, but a part of them wanted this coversation to be a little bit more longer. Both of them, waiting for the other one to interupt. But when it did'nt happened, Radhi finally spoke

" So , see you there then "

" Yup, See you"

And she hunged up.

From that moment onwards, it felt like it was much longer for a day. He tried flipping through his books, listening music but nothing really helped. He hadn't found himself this much eager in years. His eyes continuously peeked at the clock and he wanted it to be 4 everytime he looked at it. He closed his book after reading the same pages for maybe five times but none of the times he was completely into it.

Aimlessly he went to Dadu's room and saw the man staring out of the window lying on the same bed.

" It must be very boring ", Anirudh sat on the stool near his bed.

"Well, at times it is "

" Don't worry..you'll be fine and then you can go to your evening walks ", he held Dadu's hand and touched it on his cheek.

" Why you guys speak as if something has happened to me..."

"O yes, we know you are fine as a horse "

" NO DOUBT , I AM ! "

" We can go to the terrace if you want to...you ll feel nice there "

"Oh let it be.. " Dadu sighed.

He caressed Anirudh's cheek and looked at the boy with his old but gleaming eyes.

" You are doing fine in Delhi bacche , right ? ", the depth in his voice increased.

" Of course I am, why would you ask so "

" By fine , I don't mean your studies .... I am pretty sure you must be aceing in that."

" I am "

" You have people to talk to there ; right ? "

"Arre, I have many friends. You know about Shyam "

" He is the only one I know about "

" I have other friends also , It's just that I don't like hanging out with them much ", his head slowly turned down avoiding Dadu's eyes. Dadu saw the answer to that question in his eyes and how terribly he had lied.

" Beta, you know It's important to have people in life "

" Well, I have you "

"But I won't be there always "

" You said you were fine as a horse , what about that, what's going to happen to you ? "

" Not now, but someday, like everybody else, I ll also have to accept the truth of our mortal lives. And I will have no regrets at the moment. I had a very good time here. The only thing that I feel afraid of is that you being left alone after me. It won't be fair to you bacche. Your life has revolved around me since your parents left and I don't want it to continue being that way even after I am not there. "

His eyes got wet as he completed the sentence. The words left Anirudh numb. Of course he knew that Dadu was not always going to be with him but hearing all this from him was a rather different experience for him too.

He got up and hugged Dadu as tight as he could and they stayed same for a while.

CHAPTER SEVEN

An unpleasant memory

Dadu's concern was very much obvious. After his parents, the boy rarely interacted. There was even a time when he used to lock himself in his room, wrapped around his mother's stall. He used to spend the whole day like this. It took Dadu a great time to take him out of the web he had spun for himself. He saw the kid loosing his childhood and therefore decided to put all the efforts to make him feel loved. He did all he could to lessen his sorrows and it seemed he succeded too.Dadu gave him the direction which he almost lost and taught him the ways of life and the ironies involved. Anirudh also did his best as a learner and tried to adapt everything his grandfather told him too. He did great in high school and completed his boards with distinction. It was only a matter of time, when Dadu realised that the company of his uncle and aunt would do no good to the boy's fragile state of mind and hence decided to send him to Delhi. Keeping the apple of his eyes away from him was nothing but heartbreaking for Dadu himself. But he also knew staying in Gwalior was not benificial for him in any manner. The day he broke the news to Anirudh , he knew he is going to hate him for this and would ask a number of questions and maybe he would not have answers to all of them but it turned out to be rather opposite. Anirudh just looked at Dadu with a blanked face and not a single word came out of his mouth. but the silence itself was deafning. It was something that Dadu was not prepared for. Anirudh was once again seperated from someone he wanted to be with. Although Dadu proved to be a very good teacher but he couldn't be the companion which he wanted him to be. Somewhere Dadu knew that inspite everything he does, he could never fill the void within him.

The days in engineering college made him more competetive and focused.The first semester was basically getting up everyday morning and going to classes; then coming back to his room. Unlike other students, he didn't roamed around the cafeterias. Always in his books, he did'nt bothered about anyone or anything else. Soon, he met Shyam who was pretty much of the same kind and perhaps that was the reason of their friendship. No matter how busy, he managed to call Dadu almost every alternate days. He usually avoided parties and said they were just a waste of time but this one time he went to one. It was a birthday party of a senior, whom he did not knew. It was just that the invitaion was forwarded in the college groups and it was compulsory for every receiver to attend it. Since, Shyam was gone to his uncle's for some work, Anirudh had to go there by himself.

The atmosphere was lively. Everybody seemed to have a great time. The menu consisted of a variety of items. Some of them were even difficult to pronounce. Anirudh felt like an outcast who didn't belonged there. Hence, he just stood in a corner and tried to avoid everyone. The only thing that cherished him was the cuisine and the fact that people were avoiding it to remain engaged in useless gossips annoyed him. But again, he didn't had enough social confidence to just take a plate and start eating before others so he chose to just wait. He took out his earphones and plugged them in. Played a song and everything else got mute.

It was his way of taking a break from the hectic world and he often did this when he needed to cut out from his surroundings. His favourite songs in his ears were his temporary escape. Whenever in a pensive mood , it helped him to lighten up things. Some sort of magic he believed. While he was deep down the lanes of the music he felt a slight touch on his back as if someone patted him. He opened his eyes and turned around.

There stood a girl , undoubtedly attractive smiling at him. He quickly took out the earphones and replied.

"Yes ? "

" Anirudh? Right ? "

"Yes I am...."

" Nandini.. Second Year" she said, extending her hand towards him. They shook.

"So.what can I do for you?" asked Anirudh.

" Is it necessary to talk only if there's some need? " she replied raising her left eyebrow.

"No...I mean do I know you ? "

"No dear you don't...but I do..Infact I was looking forward to have this conversation from weeks"

"Sorry? "

"Oh..you don't need to be...finally we meet. Actually you were right, there's something I want "

" What's that ? "

" Thermodynamics...you are good in that....I need you to teach me "

" Ohkay I mean..I can try "

"It's done then!! You're going to teach me . I ll tell you the place "

Before he could speak any further she handed him a piece of paper with a phone number on it.

"Give me a call , then we'll schedule " she said and She walked out of the gate while speaking.

Nandini had this dominating aura around her. Completely opposite to Anirudh's. There are people who can have a personality can leave an impact just in their first meet, Nandini belonged to that kind. She owned the conversation so much that he had no other choice but to agree to her proposal.

A day was chosen and their meeting was scheduled at Nandini's PG. It was still, a bit unconvincing for Anirudh that a girl like her had spared an evening for him, even though it was for studying but still it was something that most of the boys in his hostel would have fought for.

Anirudh was there on time, he gave a her a call as he was told to and then patiently waited for her in the lobby. After a couple of minutes Nandini came downstairs looking for him. She still looked as pretty as she was in that party. He wondered if she ever put her make-up off. Anyways, they went up in her room. Her room was a typical girl's room. As in everything was properly placed as if they were never been touched. The curtains were clean and tidely wrapped . The shelves contained few books but decently arranged.

"So, you like it ? ", Nandini said

Anirudh stopped looking around her room and turned towards her.

"Yeah, I mean it's beautiful. "

"Well, it's the way I keep it ", she started moving around a few books from the shelf and took out one of them.

"Thermodynamics...well here you go! " , she handed it to him.

"So, shall we start ? ", Anirudh asked politely

"Sure", she replied.

And they sat by her study table and he started going through her book.

"It's kind of hot in there, isn't it?" she murmured

"Well...it is the season....."Before he could speak any further she, took out her cardigan which she was wearing over her top and kept it aside."

"Better..." she said.

The atmosphere turned very awkward for Anirudh and he quickly buried his hed in the book trying to tell himself that it's all normal.

"So...shall we begin with the first one ?" Anirudh asked.

"Well...from wherever you like", Nandini replied in a heavy tone.

Ignoring her tone, he started going through the chapter and after a minute he started the explanation.

"So...you see here they have started with the basic definition...." as he spoke, he felt that Nandini had moved a bit closer to his chair. Whatever was happening in the room was heavily uncomfortable for him but he was too shy to speak anything as he thought that he might be the one taking wrong signals. But Nandini was no where near understanding his situation and she continued leaning towards him.

There came a point when she came so close to him that he could feel her breath on his cheek. That was it for him, he could not bear that anymore. He pushed the table and got up with a jolt.

"What's wrong with you !!" , he almost shouted.

"I told you he's not going to", he heard a voice from his back. As he turned around, he saw two boys coming out of the cupboard. One of them was Anshuman Sharma, Nandini's batch mate and the other one was unknown to

him.
" He doesn't have the balls to do so ", said the other guy handing a 500 rupee note to Anshuman.
Before Anirudh could figure what the hell was going on. Nandini stood up and said, " Aaareee yaaar!! 2 minutes more and I would've won the bet. "
"Yeah yeah, ", Anshuman mocked her , keeping the note in his backpocket
The three of them started having a little quarrel among themselves while Anirudh stood in a corner trying to understand the scenario.
"Oh, you poor thing, still don't know what happened" ,said the other boy.
"Sorry bro, we put a tiny bet that I can make any guy kiss me", Nandini cleared it.
"Why me then? " , Anirudh asked confused.
"Well, you just happened to be there and we chose you ", Anshuman replied.
"I almost did it! " Nandini exclaimed.
"Well, there was nothing like 'almost' mentioned in the bet ", Anshuman teased her.
Anirudh didn't know how to respond to all this, should he be angry? But what will he achieve by doing so. He felt like an absolute idiot who cannot see this coming. After all, how come a girl , pretty like her would ask him out; even if it is for studying. They'd prefer idiots like Anshuman who are way more muscular and handsome than he would ever be. He should have trusted his instincts. He was more furious on his own self than on them. Drenched in humiliation, he ran away from there and vowed not to stop before his room. The evening only added more miseries to his college life. He could hear people talking behind his back. "The boy who got pranked by seniors". There were rumors that he

was the first to make an attempt on kissing Nandini and she was the one who resisted, saying it was a prank. The gossips ran by the ears of Shyaam too, but he never asked him, what exactly happened that day.

CHAPTER EIGHT

Is it a date?

He came back to his room, still thinking about Dadu's words "It's important to have people in life. " He knew what he meant, He wanted to tell Dadu about his newly accquired friend and that he was going to spend some time with her but he also didn't wanted to jinx it by telling out loud.

He thought that he will tell him once he is back home. Amidst all this, it was 3:37 , time to leave.

On his way to the bus stop, the whole city looked more colourful to him, as if somebody had added more joyful and vibrant shades. It was rather his nervousness or excitement that he wore a full black tshirt on a hot sunny day. Inspite of this, the sun had no effect on him. He was as comfortable as one would be on a breezy morning. He reached the bus stop, paid the rickshaw wala. and moved his eyes in search of her. There she was, at the same spot where he had seen her for the first time. It was only their second meeting, but to him it felt as if she was known to him since ages. On a scale of 1 to 10 she looked like a glorious infinity.

She waved at him and he waved back.

" I've been here since half an hour", she said.

" But you said we have to be here till 4 ? ", he replied confused

"Was it?", she looked up

"Yeah"

"Then it's fine, I guess. Never mind " she smiled.

" So what's the plan Mister ?", she asked.

Minutes later both of them were in a bus for the Gwalior Fort. Since, they managed to find only one vacant seat, Anirudh offered Radhika to sit and he stood beside her holding the bar. The journey was very bumpy. It felt as if the driver had chosen the most uneven route. At times, the jerks almost made him fall but he stood there somehow. Radhika on the other hand enjoyed his struggle. After some time, Radhika offered Anirudh her place but Anirudh's male ego rejected the fact that a girl will be standing while he'd enjoy the comfortable seat.

"Fair enough ! " , Radhika said and continued enjoying the sight.

After an hour, they reached their destination. The bus dropped them on the other side of the road. As they were about to cross, Anirudh stopped suddenly.

" Shit!!" , Anirudh exclaimed

"What happened now ?"

"Don't tell me today is a tuesday!"

"What if I say so?"

"They have a day off on Tuesdays"

"Seriously! Are you kidding me... "

" I was so excited that I forgot "

" Yaar! that's not done"

" Okay I know I screwed up, but right now we really need to step aside from the middle of the road"

"Okay but if we've come till here, we are going to check at least" Radhika said and crossed the road annoyed.

" There you go! see, I said they have a day off", Anirudh said. He sounded a bit rejoiced by knowing that he was

right.
"Why did'nt you came up with this before, we boarded the bus". Radhika said and sat on a bench beside.
"See, I am sorry, I told you I was excited and I have came here after a long time and ..." Anirudh continued with his explaination and. He sounded like a pre-school kid, explaining his teacher that why was his home-work incomplete. Radhika stared at his face as he blabbered. All of a sudden, she chuckled. She found his fussing to be funny.

"Okay, okay , stop crying. I am not going to punish you", she interrupted.

" Of course you won't", Anirudh said with a bit of confusion.

"So, you have done your part, now I have to be the saviour of this date". Radhika said

" Date? Did you just say this is a date? ", Anirudh's face turned bright.

"Okay, so moving ahead, we are here to see the fort , So we will see it. ", Radhika stated

"Did'nt you hear whatever I spoke to you just now", said Anirudh

" Aare Baba !! You see, those guards, that's the only security they have. "

"So...what are you implementing here? ", Anirudh's confusion increased Radhika smiled and winked at him.

"Come with me" , She held his hand and dragged him behind her.

Soon they reached a spot where the fencing was quite short and it was also not in the guards' sight. Radhika looked at Anirudh and pointed at the fencing. The strange light in her eyes was stating her notorious intentions.
She hopped and climed a boundary which was smaller than

the rest of them. Anirudh stood behind her trying to learn. He was quite astonished seeing her skills. Radhika sat on the top and lended her hand to him, indicating him to climb. Anirudh pulled his trousers and folded the sleeves of his shirt and started with his struggle.One could easily tell that he was having a hard time trying to climb.

"Seriously ? You don't know how to climb a wall", Radhika said.

"Well they don't teach you that!"

" Stop making excuses and be a man"

Radhika took hold of his hand and pulled Anirudh up. They both sat on the top of the wall He was just gaining his breath when she took a jump and landed inside the campus. Anirudh did the same but he did'nt landed on his feet.

"See you did something you've never done before

"So, what are we doing now ?", Anirudh asked with excitement

" I haven't thought that yet" Radhika laid down in the green grass bed and stretched her legs and arms.

" Hey, We are in now! Let's see the fort ...", Anirudh said

" This seems fine.", Radhika said closing her eyes.

" This? Did we crossed the fence to take a sunbath? "

" Think it as enjoying what you just achieved. Just like warriors when they win a battle! Don't they dance and celebrate? Just like that only, this is our celebration."

"Ohkay... " Anirudh chuckled and laid down like her.

It was around 6:25 and the dusk had just arrived. The sky looked beautiful as it carried away the fading warmth of the sun and was preparing for the tenderness of the moon. Their was a peculiar sense of relaxtion inside Anirudh, something he had not felt in years. It was like passing a difficult exam without studying, or like just like when you are not feeling like going to work and someone reminds you that today is a holiday. Something like that. He slowly turned his head and looked at Radhika, as she lied there with her eyes closed. He wondered if she felt the same as him.

He was wandering in the lanes of his own thoughts when he heard his phone ringing. He pulled it out from his pocket and picked it up, it was his uncle.

Radhika opened her eyes as he said hello on the phone and looked at him. She saw his face turning pale as if he had heard that the world was about to end. Panic rushed his inner self. His hands clenched, eyebrows reduced and he started sweating. Radhika got up and held his hand.

"WHAT HAPPENED? " she asked

CHAPTER NINE

An Unexpected Turn

He still had his cell phone on his ears and inaudible sounds were coming from the other end, but Anirudh got numb. He looked at Radhika and tried to say something but words refused to come out of his mouth.

"I NEED TO GO", He stammered and sprinted towards the main gate. Perhaps his disturbed mind made him forget that they were intruders and that they were the last thing that the guards at the gate expected. He just ran to get out of there. Radhika followed him instantly and she was trying to come up with answers to the assumed questions that the guards were going to ask them.

When they were about some metres away from the exit. Radhika saw the faces of the two guards standing at the entrance which happened to be the exit too. They seemed confused rather than angry or annoyed. Radhika yelled "We are sorry" when they passed the guards and continued behind Anirudh. Unlike her assumptions the guards were quiet and just gave them killing looks. Maybe because they were not the first one to tresspass in the fort and the guards were kind of got used too of this. Anirudh stopped at the road and turned towards her. He held her hands tightly.

" I... I need to go to the hospital... Uncle called..."

"But what happened"

"Dadu.... Dadu ... He .. he is not well.. I have to go"
"Ohkay.. but what happened to him?"
"I don't know.... I need to be with him.. I'll I'll get you a cab"
Radhika had not seen Anirudh like this before. He seemed to be the calmest person she ever met. Also he was the one who helped her calm down when they first met. Seeing him so much disturbed, she knew that no matter what, He shouldn't be left alone right now.
"I 'll come with you..", Radhika stated
"No, you don't need to... " He said while impatiently looking for a ride.
"No...I do!!" Radhika argued.
Anirudh looked at her and then looked at the empty road in front of them.
"Okay.. I guess we need to go by ourselves only.."
"That's fine, let's go!"

Anirudh was running on the streets like crazy. He didn't cared about his surroundings or what the people looking at him thought. He would take a stop just to have a look at Radhika and then continued his sprint once he made sure she was fine. In that moment, he just wanted to reach the hospital as soon as he could. There was a bunch of different emotions quarreling inside him. Of course he was worried, but he felt angry at the same time. Angry with the ways of the world. His breath was getting short but he ran like he is the only own who can save Dadu. Radhika ran behind him. Her part was more hectic because she was also trying to look for any autos on the way but was unable to find any. She marathoned behind Anirudh.

Once they reached the hospital, cold air rushed down Anirudh's spine.... Radhika walked a few steps behind him and watched him as he peeped inside every room and hall they crossed.... She made his work easier and reached out to the reception. At, the reception, they had this lady who seemed to be the most annoyed and busy person in the entire world; she graciously ignored all the chaos around her.... and was busy in her own petty task of brushing her nails with a little knife... Radhika slammed the desk with her hand in order to bring the lady's atttention towards her.

"Can you please look for Mr. Kashyap?", Radhika pleaded.

The lady looked at Radhika with dead eyes and was simply not happy with her for distracting her from her busy schedule. Still, she did her the favor and scrolled her finger down a sturdy looking register.

"OT, Second floor", she replied with a straight voice without looking at Radhika's face....

Anirudh ran towards the second floor as soon as these words came out from the lady's mouth. Radhika took her turn of displaying arrogance and decided to move forward without thanking the lady...which she probably wouldn't have done with anyone else.

On the second floor, It was Anirudh's uncle who was the first one to receive him.... He held his shoulders and tried to wrap him around his arms, but Anirudh refused it and made his way towards the OT door... His heart sank a little with every step he took forward. He had sensed the worst in the atmosphere around him... near the door... stood his aunt; who stepped aside to make way for him so that he could peep in throught the glass of the OT door.... Anirudh reached the door but was not able to gather the courage to look through.... his subcontious was already aware of what had happened.... he knew it was too late...

Radhika stood near the stairs... across the hallway from Anirudh, she looked at his face and instantly knew that the thing he feared the most had happened... Dadu was no more....

Anirudh fell down on his knees, his eyes blurred but he did'nt let any of the tears fall down... He held them back...

To be continued....

9 798886 419924

Printed by Libri Plureos GmbH in Hamburg, Germany